LITTLE SIMON
An imprint of Simon & Schuster Children's Publishing Division
1230 Avenue of the Americas, New York, New York 10020
Text copyright © 2012 by Alison Reynolds
Illustrations copyright © 2012 by Heath McKenzie
First published in Australia by The Five Mile Press 2012
First Little Simon hardcover edition 2013
LITTLE SIMON is a registered trademark of Simon & Schuster, Inc.,
and associated colophon is a trademark of Simon & Schuster, Inc.
For information about special discounts for bulk purchases, please
contact Simon & Schuster Special Sales at 1-866-506-1949 or
business@simonandschuster.com.
The Simon & Schuster Speakers Bureau can bring authors to your
live event. For more information or to book an event contact the
Simon & Schuster Speakers Bureau at 1-866-248-3049 or visit
our website at www.simonspeakers.com.
Manufactured in China 0513 FMP
First Edition 10 9 8 7 6 5 4 3 2 1
ISBN 978-1-4424-8105-3
Library of Congress Cataloging-in-Publication Data
Reynolds, Alison, 1962-
A year with Marmalade / by Alison Reynolds ; illustrated by Heath McKenzie.
— 1st Little Simon ed.
pages cm
"First published in Australia by The Five Mile Press 2012."
Summary: A cat and a young girl slowly become friends when someone they love
moves away.
ISBN 978-1-4424-8105-3 (hardcover picture book) [1. Friendship—Fiction.
2. Cats—Fiction. 3. Moving, Household—Fiction.] I. McKenzie, Heath, illustrator.
II. Title.
PZ7.R3334Ye 2013
[E]—dc23
2012036437

a year
with
marmalade

ALISON REYNOLDS • HEATH McKENZIE

LITTLE SIMON

New York London Toronto Sydney New Delhi

Ella and Maddy were **best friends.**

But

one

autumn

day . . .

everything changed.

"We're going away for a year," said Maddy.
"Could you please look after Marmalade?"

Ella cried
and Marmalade yowled
as Maddy's family car grew

smaller

and

smaller

in the distance.

Ella
SCRUNCHED
and
toSsed
the fallen leaves,

but nobody
tossed them
back.

She picked **apples,** but there were **too many** for one person to crunch. When she offered Marmalade an apple, he batted it away.

She
ST

OMPED

through puddles,

but she was the only
one who got wet.

One
frosty
winter's morning,
Ella woke up with **warm feet**.

The pond
FROZE
OVER,

and Ella *sped around* on her skates.

SHIVERING

high up in the tree,
Marmalade gazed at her
with diamond eyes.

The days became
even colder,
and Ella stayed inside.

Marmalade **swished** around Ella's legs as she read beside the fire.

In spring Ella dug up a garden bed.

Marmalade scratched up the seeds and purred.

Ella

planted
a row

of
flowers.

Marmalade curled up on the sun-warmed earth.

One morning Ella
found a **huge** sunflower.

"**Come and look**, Marmalade!"

she shouted.

Marmalade **darted** out.

That summer

Ella and Marmalade
pedaled to the beach.

They built sand castles **bigger** than Marmalade.
Ella swam while Marmalade minded the clothes.

Soon Autumn
returned ...

and so did Maddy.

Ella, Maddy, and Marmalade
SCRUNCHED
through fallen leaves.

And SPLASHED through

puddles all the way home...

Ella's dad built

a special cat flap:

between

Ella and Maddy's

homes.

It was just big enough

for Marmalade.

And Ella and Maddy.